Read more about Al's crazy adventures in:

Operation Kick Butt

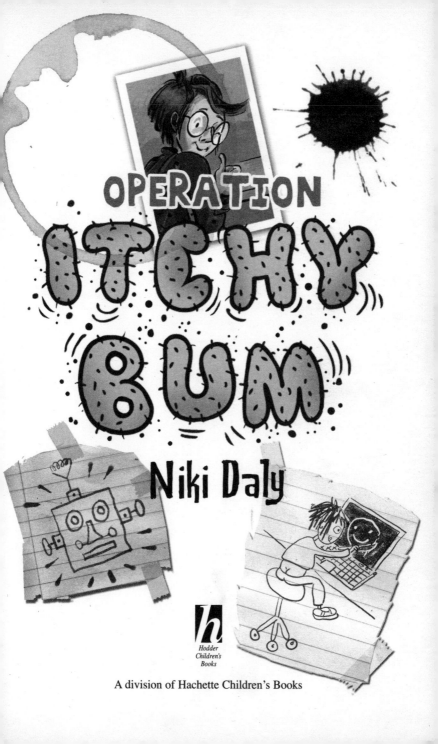

OPERATION ITCHY BUM

Niki Daly

Hodder
Children's
Books

A division of Hachette Children's Books

For Joe

Chapter One

If I had any say in the matter, I'd be called James … James Bond, even Bernie Bond. But as it happens, my name's Alistair. You can call me Al – Dad does. Mum says there's no sense wasting a good name, so she calls me Alistair, and sometimes 'Alistair D'Arcy McDermott' when she's got something important to say to me, like –

'Alistair D'Arcy McDermott, your dad and I have decided to call it a day and go our separate ways. You're coming with me.'

That was a year ago – one lousy year ago when my dad and mum separated.

'Bye, Al my Pal,' I hear Dad say. 'And remember, it's not your fault that your mother and I are splitting up. It's just that there are times when grown-ups need to go their separate ways.'

Whew! There I was thinking that I had driven him away by:

Painting Mr Smiley on his laptop screen when I turned five.

Playing with the handbrake in the Lake District when I turned seven.

Failing my annual eye test when I turned nine.

… and worst of all,

The time I faked my first tomato sauce death scene in the shower.

There were others,
but that one was the best.

Mum and I live in a block of flats called
La Range. It should be called De
Ranged because the toilet flush
causes the water pipes to
rattle, which causes Mrs
Newhardt's cat to leap two
floors on to Phelps, the
gardener, who sprays into
Creepy Mr Freedlander's

apartment, causing Creepy Mr Freedlander to use language that Mum says is not fit for my ears. Hah!

After they split up, Dad got himself a one-bedroom flat with a 'C' view. He looks straight into the second 'C' of a giant Coca-Cola sign.

At night it makes the flat glow like a night club. It's cool … in a grotty way.

Another cool thing about spending weekends with my dad is his cooking. He's the world's worst cook. So we eat stacks of takeaways. Dad read an article that claims there's no such thing as 'junk food'. Only food that tastes like junk – the kind he cooks. So he doesn't.

My dad's a bit of a brilliant slob. The kind of guy who farts about in his pyjamas (I mean, literally major butt-burpers!) over weekends, while reading technical books, making sketches and writing notes. Mum says he's a bit of a Leonardo da Vinci – all work, no play. Mum's different. She loves going out and having a good time. Dad says she a 'people's person'. Maybe that's why they split up. Dad's not a 'people', he's a person – a nice, odd sort of nerdy man person.

A lot of my friends' parents are divorced. Some of them sound mental. Like a boy in my class, Neal Downe. I swear, that's his name! Well, when Neal's dad fetches him for a weekend, he's not allowed in Neal's mum's house. He has to stand on the doorstep. It can be hailing golf balls and the poor dude has to stand outside. Sophie Ross's mum won't even let her dad see her because he has a young girlfriend who's a real babe. My mum and dad aren't like that. I mean, just because you don't love someone any more doesn't mean that you HATE them, right?

'Your mother loves you more than anything else in the world,' my dad always tells me.

'There's not a thing your father wouldn't do for you,' is what my mum always says.

That's cool. But the best thing they could *both* do for me is to pause … rewind … and start all over again.

'Wake up and smell the poo, Al!' is what my best friend, Sophie, always tells me when I mention 'the separation'. I think she means 'coffee' – which means I should get real. Well, there's something I want to tell you. I don't give up that easily … as you'll soon see!

Chapter Two

I go to Obz – Observatory Prep. The school is in the grounds of an old unused observatory, famous for having discovered a pimple on the face of an obscure planet. Now the old observatory is used for music lessons.

I play the bagpipes. Well, it was either that, violin, recorder, guitar or piano. And the only reason that such a crazy instrument is included is because it forms part of the school's badge. 'Perseverance', our motto, is especially needed to play the bagpipes. I'd add 'craziness'. I like to imagine that I am squeezing the life out of Mrs Newhardt's cat while I'm practising. Very good for relieving stress!

My best teacher is Miss Merchant. She looks like Barbie with brains. Miss Merchant could be a famous actress. When she reads *Babe* to us she does the voices, accents and all, and lets us do the sound effects.

'OINK! GRUNT! OINK!' we all go. It's so coooool.

The teacher from the fiery depths of hell is Mr Burke – Burke the Jerk. He wears tight white trousers and open-necked shirts that show off his big ape chest to the world. He thinks he's so cool. But he's a sarcastic dork who enjoys humiliating kids in front of everyone.

'It's better to be thought a fool, than open your mouth and remove all doubt,' he says to anyone who makes a mistake during his stupid history quizzes. He also has a habit of standing astride with one leg resting on a chair so that his trousers tighten over his butt. It's so disgusting.

So that's it — separated parents, wacko school with a teacher from heaven and one from hell.

Oh, and my best friend, Sophie. I told you about her, didn't I?

I've known Sophie since we were at playgroup. We carried the same cute Noddy suitcases packed with nappies. Sophie once stuck her finger up Benjy the class gerbil's bottom and made it squeak.

She's like that – she wants to know how things work.

We have a lot to talk about, Sophie and I, because I'm also very curious about things. Such as:

Q: Why do farts smell worse in the bathtub?

A: Because the gas molecules are sealed in bubbles instead of having lots of air to spread out in. *That's why!*

Quite fascinating, really.

Sophie's got this wicked laugh. When she really gets going it sounds like a squeaky toy with hiccups. I love to make her laugh just to hear her. Especially in Burke the Jerk's class.

'Sophie Ross, when you've done your impression of a hyena,' says Mr Burke, 'perhaps you can do one of a box, and shut up.'

See? Nasty!

Sophie and I share lifts. Mondays and
Tuesdays, Mum lifts. Wednesdays and Thursdays,
Mrs Ross lifts. On Fridays we take the bus to
school and my dad fetches, because after
dropping Sophie off, we go to his place for the
weekend. Sometimes, we collect Sophie on a

Saturday or Sunday and do something special – like visit the science museum, go to the cinema, or walk around a park.

Once, while we were looking at a group of swans, Dad told us how male and female swans stay together for life.

'They're better than people,' said Sophie. We all kept quiet and watched as the mama and papa swan glided side by side followed closely by their baby cygnets.

'Lucky duckys!' said Sophie.

Chapter Three

We're in the back of the car talking about Burke the Jerk. Mrs Ross says, 'Come now, that's no way to talk about a teacher.'

'Torturer, you mean,' says Sophie. 'He's given us a 3D map of Europe to do before next Monday. He wants us to do mountains and rivers. That means we will have to work the whole weekend.'

Sophie puts her finger into her mouth and does a pretend vomit on to the backseat. I pretend to eat it up. That sends her into a fit of giggles.

'Honestly, you'd laugh if the cat's bottom was on fire,' says Mrs Ross. We laugh our sides sore, until I fall out on to the pavement outside La Range.

When I tell Mum that I've got a weekend project to do, she says, 'In that case, it's best you don't go to your dad's. You're going to need a lot of space to work in. I'll ask Gran to come over and help you.'

'What about you?' I ask.

'You know I can't even build a sandcastle without it collapsing,' she explains weakly. 'Besides, I have a blind date.'

I almost choke on the breakfast cereal I'm having for supper.

'Whaaa?' I say, not believing my ears.

'A blind date,' she repeats. 'Aunt Fran has set me up with a blind date. You might know him.

16

He teaches at Obz.'

Before I can close my mouth she does it
again – shocks the daylights out of me.

'Graham Burke.'

'Whaaat! Burke the Jerk! That's revolting!' I
shout so loudly that she has to cover her ears.

When she removes her hands, she says,
'Alistair D'Arcy McDermott, there is no
need to be disrespectful.'

'But Mum,' I start explaining, 'he's not
very nice.'

'Aunt Fran's boyfriend, Clive, knows him
quite well from their sports club. He says
Mr Burke is very sociable, a good dancer, a
neat dresser and a member of Mensa. He's
supposed to have an amazingly high IQ.'

'He has the IQ of a demented dork,' I say.

'Well, I need to go out and get a life,' says
Mum, tearfully.

'What about meeeeeeeeee?' I wail, hoping Mrs Newhardt will think I'm being abused and call the cops.

Instead, I see her cat sail past our window.

Chapter Four

Gran arrives with a basket full of stuff. Gran's an artist. She paints gigantic naked ladies with powerful legs – 'Thunder Thighs', she calls them. They're fun, and she sells her paintings for millions.

She's going to show me how to make Europe in papier mâché. We start by cutting small strips of newspaper. Gran mixes a bowl of wallpaper paste while I copy the map of Europe on to a board. I'm not bad at drawing, actually. Then we build up the land masses and mountains using some clay. After that, we start putting strips of sticky newspaper over the clay.

'Don't you like getting your hands all gunged up?' says Gran. 'It's so earthy!' Soon the sloppy mess starts looking like Europe.

'Italy is my favourite country,' says Gran, patting it into shape. 'Such gorgeous men!'

I laugh, but it reminds me of Mum's blind date. What's the opposite of gorgeous … GROSS! I tell Gran what a gross, tacky dork Mum's going on a blind date with.

'Your mum needs to get out a bit,' says Gran. 'Don't be so hard on her.' I give her my miserable, neglected, unloved look and she squeezes me tight. She smells of oil paint and something called 'Midnight Sin'.

Just then, Mum comes in holding a slinky black dress up to her chest.

'What do you think, Mum?' she asks Gran.

'Dead sexy,' says Gran.

'Too much show?' asks Mum.

'Maybe, for a first date,' says Gran.

I swear, if Mum goes on a second date with Burke the Jerk, I'll run away. I imagine myself fleeing across France into Italy. My fingers skip across the Alps.

'Hey!' says Gran. 'You're flattening the Matterhorn.'

Gran says we should let Europe dry and go for a walk.

It's a hot day and Phelps is watering a flower bed.

I notice him giving Gran the eye.

'He can keep his shoes under my bed, any time,' says Gran, giving me a naughty wink.

I give her a push and run ahead.

In the park, she says to me, 'You've really had a tough time, haven't you?'

It's the first time I want to cry. I've had to be so brave for Mum and Dad. But now, I don't have to. Gran puts her arm around me and I feel tears well up in the corners of my eyes.

'I know,' says Gran, 'I know.'

But I wonder if she really does know how horrible it is not to be together any more. And if Mum starts going on blind dates and gets married again, we'll NEVER EVER be together EVER AGAIN. I lean against Gran, leaving a wet patch on her blouse.

When we return, Europe still feels like a bog. Italy is all lumpy and soft, and Greece has spread like porridge into the Adriatic.

'Don't worry,' says Gran, 'it'll be dry tomorrow and look amazing with a bit of paint.'

Mum is taking her beauty sleep before her date, so Gran and I play a few rounds of Trivial Pursuit. I've played it so many times that I know just about all the answers.

'Who invented the word "robot"?'

'The Czech author Karel Čapek,' I answer.

'You're amazing,' says Gran. 'I only know about art and film stars. Your mum says Mr Burke is quite a mastermind.'

'He's a Master Muckhead,' I say. 'He only knows what he reads from his notes. And even then he gets things wrong. He called President Obama "Obama Ben Laden". And when Julius Pettifer, who's a real genius, told him that Osama Bin Laden was an international terrorist, and Barack Obama is the American President, he ordered him out of the class for disrupting the lesson. Duh?'

'Well, I hope he's nice company for your mum tonight,' says Gran, getting up to start dinner.

Gran makes the most amazing eggy-bread. After she dips slabs of white bread in egg, she dips them into rice crispies and then into a pan of sizzling butter. Insane! I like pouring syrup over mine, but I am only allowed one sweet one, after one with baked beans and bacon. Only, I don't eat bacon any more, after I got to know a pig called Cyril really well. He lives in the city farm near us, and is SO intelligent. He knows how to open and close gates and peel a banana. He eats the peel afterwards! He's very neat and delicate about it.

Come to think of it, I'd MUCH rather Mum was going on a blind date with old Cyril. At least he has an excuse for being a pig!

★

The bell rings as we are packing dishes into the dishwasher. But before we can get it, Mum beats us to the door and waves us a goodbye kiss.

'Not too late, Alistair,' she orders. And then to Gran, 'Don't let him watch any junk on telly, Mum! He's got a wild enough imagination as it is.'

'OK, Miss Control-Freak!' jokes Gran. 'Go, go! Before the lipstick smudges!'

As soon as Mum shuts the door, Gran and I rush to the window to see her and her blind date drive off. Burke the Jerk is all decked out in white. He looks like Disco Ken.

'Funny,' says Gran. 'The van that has been parked all afternoon across the road has just sped off behind your mum and Mr Burke, like a scene from one of those mad movies where everyone chases up everyone else's behind.'

I peer out and see the van as it screeches around the corner.

'I think it's one of those vans that looks for people who haven't paid their TV licence,' I tell Gran.

'Really?'

'Yes, it had a dish on the roof.'

'Has your mum got a TV licence?' asks Gran, all concerned.

'Guess so,' I say.

'Good, then let's go and watch some junk,' says Gran, hauling me into the lounge.

Chapter Five

It's Sunday and Mum comes into the kitchen looking whacked.

'So?' asks Gran.

'So … so-so,' says Mum. She's unsure. Good!

'Tell, tell!' says Gran, pulling up her sleeves. She wants to hear it all. And she wants it NOW! I leave the room, but stay within snooping distance. I hear Mum describe her blind date.

'He's not bad-looking. He looks like that guy

who acted in … what was that movie called?'

'Freddy in *A Nightmare on Elm Street*,' I suggest, loudly.

'Oh, shut up in there,' Mum responds, and to Gran she says, 'He's Tom Cruise … ish.'

'He's nothing like Tom Cruise,' I say, unable to stay out of it. 'Plus he whitens his teeth and Sophie says he wears a hair extension.'

'Oh, rubbish,' says Mum. 'I know real hair when I see it!'

'So he's perfect?' asks Gran.

'Almost,' says Mum.

I'm all ears. Gran leans forward, waiting to hear the next titbit.

'He cracks his knuckles,' says Mum. 'Other than that, he's perfect.'

I want to vomit. My own mother!

Gran says, 'So you'll see him again?'

'We'll see,' says Mum, and giggles.

I don't say a word. I just glare at Mum with my unhappy-chappy look.

'I'm not saying I will,' she says nervously, and changes the subject.

When I tell Sophie that Mum went on a date with our worst enemy she says, 'I wondered why Burke the Jerk was sucking up to you today.' She's right. He has been. Gave me an A plus for my map – says it's very nicely 'textured'.

He has also started calling me 'Al', which really sucks. *That's Dad's name for me.* But I really begin to worry when class breaks up for the day and he says, 'See you later, Al.'

When I get home from school, Mum says, 'We're eating out tonight. Graham's treating us to pizza.'

I go, like: 'Huh?!'

'Isn't that nice of him?'

I turn my eyes up and give them a roll.
'Noooooo!'

'Oh, don't be like that!' says Mum, going off
to take a long bath.

★

When Burke the Jerk arrives to pick us up he says, 'Mmmm, you smell nice.'

And he doesn't mean me! I've decided NOT to wash. And I'm wearing my old 'You Suck!' sweater. It has a bit of cheese from my last pizza still stuck to it.

'Hi, Al,' he greets me.

I let my sweater do the talking.

I'm going to make him pay ... BIG TIME!

When we get to Big Bill's Dynamite Pizzas, I order the extra large BIG BILL with double cheese, double salami, double pineapple, a sprinkle of chilli and aromate. Maybe I'll eat two slices and play with the rest.

'Aromate's full of tartrazine,' Burke the Jerk informs Mum.

Mum sighs, 'No aromate, Alistair. You know it makes you hyper.'

'The Tartrazine Kid rules!' I cry, giving the plastic tomato sauce container a good squeeze. I watch the blob, almost in slow motion, go up ... up, and PLOP! – straight towards Burke the Jerk's open-necked shirt and into his hairy forest.

'Aaaah!' he gasps, as though he's been shot through the chest. 'My shirt! It's a Leonardo La Louche pure silk!' the Big Baby sobs.

'Oh, look at what you've done!' says Mum, smearing the sauce into his chest with a napkin. She's made a right mess. Grizzly knots of hair and tomato sauce make him look like an emergency ward case. His la-la-whatever pure silk shirt is a write-off!

He glares at me across the table.

I glare straight back.

Without a further word, war has been declared.

Chapter Six

Mum's furious. She's never seen me like this before. *I've never seen myself like this before.* I'm actually a sweet person. *No, really!*

'I wouldn't be surprised if he never calls again!' she says when we get home.

Lying in bed, I wonder … what if he does? What if he's serious about her? I go to sleep with visions of myself, sword drawn, battling against a three-headed dragon in a white suit. Gran, with a tribe of Thunder Thighs, helps pin him down, while I remove each of his heads.

★

First thing the next morning, I hear Mum on the phone.

'I'm really sorry about Alistair's behaviour last night,' she says. 'He's had an awful lot to cope with since his dad and I separated.'

She listens and then says, 'Well, you're a darling for being so understanding.' Then she listens some more and says, 'Let's see. I don't think we should rush anything.'

I feel ill. When Mum comes to hurry me for school I throw up.

Uh oh! Bits of Big Bill splurge on to the floor.

'I thought you shouldn't have had such a big pizza,' Mum says, removing my top. 'Darling, I'm calling Gran. You'll have to stay in bed today.'

I'm so relieved. I couldn't bear facing Burke the Jerk. I need time to gather my forces. Draw up my battle plans. Sharpen my *Excalibur*. At least, sharpen my pencils!

Gran comes and sits at the end of my bed.

'I believe you were a monster last night,' she says, trying hard not to smile.

'Oh, Gran, it sucks!' I moan. 'Mum actually seems to like him.'

'And you?' asks Gran.

I stick a finger down my throat, but quickly pull it out again. I've nothing left to throw up. I stare blankly at the ceiling.

'Well, I'm not sure what can be done about it,' says Gran, patting my feet. 'But I'm sure you'll think of something,' she adds, getting up.

Left alone, I get out an old exercise book and write on the cover:

Plan: Secretly remove batteries from remote control

Burke gone BESERK!

Then I start designing some wicked Burke the Jerk Repellents. One, a head disposal machine, is inspired by our old bowling machine at Obz, invented by Colonel Peebles, our school's first headmaster. I fill up pages with diabolical inventions. At lunch Gran comes in.

'Feeling better?' she asks.

'Much better!' I say, managing a smile.

strategically position Burke's £300 shades in exit

FIRE!

Save me!

Our hero in a hurry to be the FIRST to escape

Stage 1

CRUNCH!

Stage 2

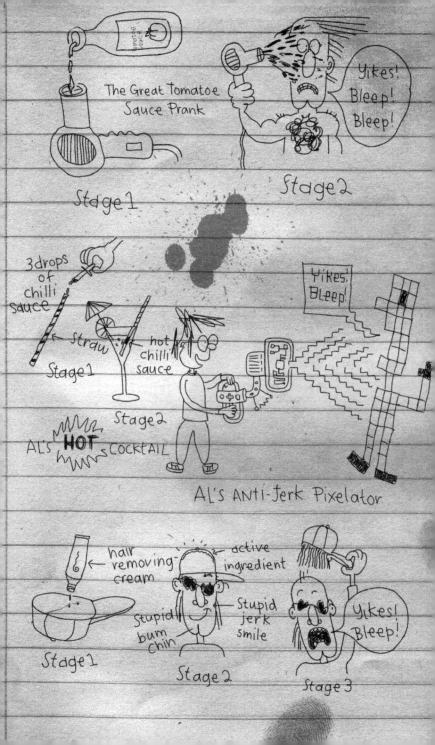

Chapter Seven

For the next few weeks the only place I see Burke the Jerk is at school. Mum doesn't mention him, and neither do I – glad for things to be normal again. Well, almost everything …

One Sunday I'm looking through our window down at the street.

'Mum, have we paid our TV licence?' I ask.

'Yes. Why?' she answers, coming over to the window to see what I'm looking at.

'Cos that van's been hanging around our street for a few weeks now,' I say.

'Which one?' she asks.

'That one, trying to stay hidden behind the large oak,' I point out.

'I've noticed it around the place,' says Mum. 'I think it might be a TV unit doing a reality show, or something.'

'Weird,' I say. 'Perhaps Mr Freedlander's a serial pet killer!'

'Oh, stop it, Alistair,' says Mum. 'You're giving me the heebie-jeebies.'

★

Then a week before the end of term Mum goes and gives *me* the heebie-jeebies!

'We're going to Graham's holiday house for a weekend,' she tells me. 'It'll give us a chance to get to know one another in a more relaxed way.'

I don't want to listen to her.

'I'll stay with Dad,' I say.

'You can't. He'll be away on business,' she says.

'I'll go to Gran's, then.'

'Gran's going to Italy.'

'I can go with her,' I bounce back. It's become like ping-pong.

'No, you can't. Gran's going with a group of old ladies,' she strikes back.

'Maybe I can stay with Sophie,' I shoot, desperately building a list of people I might be able to stay with: Miss Merchant … Mrs Newhardt … Mr Freedlander the serial killer!

'Listen, Alistair,' says Mum, forcing me to look at her. 'Graham and I have been spending time with one another for the past few weekends. We'd like to see if there's a future for us. All of us … together.'

I feel trapped. I look at Mum. She looks so sad.

Finally, I say, 'OK, then.'

She hugs me.

'You're my number one,' she says. 'Don't forget that.'

I won't. I go to my room and start preparing survival plans for my holiday in hell.

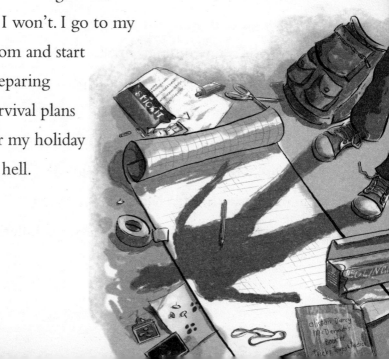

Chapter Eight

There's a week left of school before the dreaded holiday begins. The last week of term is always a bit of a party. On one day, Miss Merchant says we can come dressed as our favourite fictional characters. I squeeze my trainers into a pair of red rubber gloves and go as The Red Monkey (my fav comic anti-hero). Sophie has gone all out on her costume, but I still don't know who she's supposed to be. She keeps saying:

'Oooooooo! I absolutely love Room Service.'

But I still don't get it.

'Eloise, you dummy!' she says, finally.

Figures … it's a girls' book.

We are asked to read an extract from our character's book, but in the middle of my reading Miss Merchant gets called  out of class … by Burke the Jerk. I stop reading and study them through the door. Miss Merchant looks upset. Burke the Jerk shakes her by the shoulders. It looks as though he's trying to explain something that she can't understand. Finally, she shrugs him off and returns to the class.

'Carry on, Alistair,' she says. But I can tell that she's not really listening any more.

Something's up. Sophie's noticed it as well.

'Did you see that?' she says during break. 'Burke the Jerk made Miss Merchant cry.'

'I think they are boyfriend and girlfriend,' says Juno, who sits in our group at break.

'They're not, I've seen him chatting up a strange-looking woman in the car park,' says Simon Bates. 'He's an old *lecher*.'

I feel as though I've been stabbed through the ears with a skewer. But I don't comment. Since my mother's been seeing Burke the Jerk, I've told no one about it, except Sophie. It's just too embarrassing. But if Juno's right, I'm sure as *anything* going to tell my mum. In fact, it might be just the secret weapon that I've been looking for.

But when I do spill the beans on Burke the Jerk being a *lecher*, she says,

'Alistair D'Arcy McDermott, do you really expect me to believe the gossip of some kid in the playground?'

'But Mum, I saw it myself. He did upset Miss Merchant.'

'So?' questions Mum. 'I upset my receptionist when she drops my calls.'

'What's that got to do with it, Mum?' I ask, not getting her point.

'They work together, that's all!' says Mum.

OK, I need more evidence. I need to draw the enemy out into the open. I have a few more days to refine my plans.

The weekend before we join Burke the Jerk at his holiday home, Dad asks me,

'How're things at home?'

'Fine,' I say.

'How about school?'

'School sucks.'

'Bagpipes?'

'I'm playing at the Caber and Bagpipe Schools Festival next term.'

'Well, then I'll come,' he says.

'No,' I reply quickly. 'Er, it'll be boring.

Lots of Scottish dancing, you know … boring stuff like that.'

'So, you don't want me to come, right?'

I nod.

'Because your mum has a boyfriend, right?'

I nod.

I look him in the eye. I think he looks hurt.

'I'm still your dad,' he says. 'Right?'

'Right.'

Dad drives me home after a takeaway lunch of chilli-chicken wraps. I have to pack for my 'holiday'.

Downstairs, I watch as he and Mum say their goodbyes.

'Have a good holiday!' says Dad, climbing into his car. I notice that he gives her arm a little squeeze.

'Good luck with your business trip,' says

Mum in return. Dad leaves and I watch her standing for a while out on the pavement, looking around, as though she's expecting to see someone, or something.

'That van seems to have moved off elsewhere,' she mentions, coming in.

'Maybe Mr Freedlander's moved the body,' I say in my best horror-movie voice.

'What are you going on about?' Mum asks, looking irritated.

'Mrs Newhardt's cat gone missing.' I add another detail to a twisted story that's starting to curdle in my clotted brain.

At least it brings a smile to Mum's face.

'You're a creepy little boy, Alistair D'Arcy McDermott,' she says, giving my bottom a friendly pinch. 'Now go and pack. We've an early start tomorrow.'

Upstairs, I spread out my arsenal.

Tube of glitter glue

My collection of tomato sauce and mustard sachets

Itchy powder

Cling wrap

Stink bomb

Bottle of green food colouring

Chocky Bar
Yummy CHOC 100% nice

Gel

Cat paw rubber stamp

I pack my book containing Plans of Total Destruction, zip up, and stuff the various backpack pockets with my arsenal.

It's 15.45 and I'm packed, prepared, and ready to ship out!

Chapter Nine

We drive to the coast, not talking much. Mum
tries her best to cheer me up by telling me
some really nerdy jokes:

*Q: Why did the
computer cross the road?*

A: To get a byte to eat.

When I fail to laugh, she puts on a CD and
sings along:

'Oh, could this be love
Well, it's over now.'

Yeah ... well ... maybe ... no ... I hope so. I look at the passing scenery, running a plan through my head. I'll need a layout of the house, a total knowledge of Burke the Jerk's movements and habits ... and an escape route.

We are met by the Jerk himself when we arrive.

Mum looks surprised when she sees what he's wearing or, rather, what he's *not* wearing – he's butt-naked, except for an itsy-bitsy, teeny-weeny thong! I mean, not like Superman who wears his underpants OVER his tights. No, Burke the Jerk looks like a hairy ape in a thong!

'Welcome to *Maison par la Mer*,' he greets us, pulling in his pot belly.

'Say hello, Alistair,' Mum reminds me. But I am shocked speechless.

'Oh, don't mind me!' he says breezily, when he notices that my eyes are starting to pop out of their sockets. 'I'm a nature boy at heart. When I'm by the sea, I feel as free as a dolphin,' he explains, waving his arms to imitate a swimming dolphin.

My jaw drops. He might *feel* like a dolphin … but I'm thinking … *deep, very deeep sea species*. A squid to be exact! With that picture in place, I manage to close my mouth.

'Let me help you with that, Alistair,' he says, making a grab at my bulging backpack. 'It looks as though you're going on a survival course.'

'It certainly does,' adds Mum, trying to act naturally next to an ape man. 'What on earth have you brought with you?'

'My Barney collection,' I reply, sourly.

'Sweet!' says Burke the Jerk, putting his hand on my shoulder. I'd like to give it a good bite. Instead, I use an age-old war tactic: I smile – giving my enemy a false sense of security.

We go inside. Everything is white.

Mum says, 'How lovely! It's so … airy, Graham. I can see why you dress so … umm, coolly at the sea.'

I'm shown my room.

'You're in here,' he tells Mum, showing her a room next to mine. 'And I'm in here, if you need me,' he adds, with a slimy wink. He opens a door at the end of the passage. I make a quick mental note – no key!

I dump my things and look for the toilet. I meet him on the stairs.

'There's one downstairs, or you can use the

bathroom en suite in my room,' he tells me.
I do a three-sixty degree turn and hop back
upstairs to his bedroom. His big white shoes
are parked under his big white bed. *Why does
he need such a big bed?* I go into the bathroom
and take a leak, splashing a few drops on the
floor. I stand on the tips of my toes, open
the white medicine chest above the sink.

The usual stuff – dental floss, eye drops, talcum powder. Ah, and teeth whitening strips. While I'm reading the instructions: 'stick strip across teeth …' I catch a glimpse of Burke in the mirror and turn quickly to face him. Whew! He's put on a shirt.

'If you're looking for toothpaste,' he says, 'you'll find some on the washbasin in your room.' He smiles a thin, knowing smile – like he KNOWS what I'm up to. I'll have to be more careful.

'Thanks, Mr Burke,' I say, making a move for the door. He blocks it.

'Why don't you call me Graham?' he says quietly, menacingly, before allowing me through.

I can think of a million things to call him – *Bung-Hole*, for starters! But I smile and say, 'Thanks, Graham,' and head for my room.

It overlooks the bay. Below, there's a little jetty with a few boats tied up. If I need to, I can escape by sea.

I unpack my clothes into a chest of drawers, and put my backpack into a cupboard. I slide my book under the mattress, and sit on it for a few minutes thinking: this has to be a two-pronged attack – physical and psychological.

And it's time to launch my first mission –

Plan A: Operation Soil and Spoil

Be warned! It's DISGUSTING. But more than ever I am prepared to go to the foulest lengths to protect my mum against Burke the Jerk. I just know he's going to break her heart and give me grief.

For your information, I learnt this nasty bit of sabotage at a school camp.

All you need is:
A roll of cling wrap - which I've got
Method:
Lift the toilet seat and stretch a sheet
of cling wrap over the bowl. With the
seat down it's hard to dedect
especially for a jerk in a great rush

cling wrap

Yuck! What am I thinking! This is … just too,
too, gross.

STOP!

I go to:

Plan B: Operation Glitter Bum

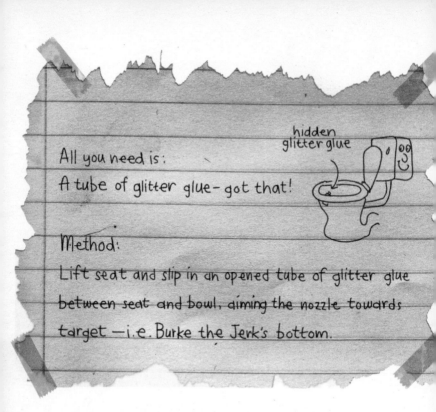

All you need is:

A tube of glitter glue - got that!

hidden glitter glue

Method:

Lift seat and slip in an opened tube of glitter glue between seat and bowl, aiming the nozzle towards target —i.e. Burke the Jerk's bottom.

Simple but *sooo* effective.

I then leave the scene of the crime.

Downstairs, I find Mum and Burke the Jerk chatting away on a big white leatherette sofa.

Mum seems to have recovered from her initial surprise at finding our host looking like Buttman.

'Graham's taking us for an early dinner tonight,' she tells me excitedly.

'What do you like to eat … besides pizza?' asks Graham, folding his legs so that his thong disappears where the sun don't shine. His bare bottom goes 'Bruuurmpff!' against the leatherette, and I see Mum's eyes widen as she shifts away from him.

'Fish fingers,' I say, '… and chips.'

'Ah, *Cuisine à la Mer*, a gourmet after my own heart,' he says sarcastically.

Mum smiles politely. She looks a bit desperate to have a good time. Still, I mustn't get all soft. I'm here on a mission.

'Want to come for a swim?' Mum asks.

'No, I'll hang around here,' I say. Burke the Jerk looks delighted with my decision.

'Give me a minute,' he says to Mum. 'Just need to visit the little boys' room!'

Mum and I wait alone as he rushes to his bathroom.

He's up there for longer than a tinkle. Excellent!

'Sure you'll be OK, love?' asks Mum.

'Yep,' I say. A couple of minutes go by.

Mum taps her foot. 'And they say that women take ages in the toilet. What's he doing up there?'

I guess he's trying to wipe up … *up there!* I think to myself.

'What are you smiling at?' Mum asks.

'Nothing … just something … a joke!'

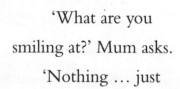

I mumble. She shakes her head and looks at me as though I'm a loony out for the weekend.

Finally, Burke the Jerk returns with a towel hanging over his shoulder … and a bum spread with glitter. When Mum catches sight of him from behind, she doubles over with laughter. I join in. Burke the Jerk twists around to see what we are laughing at and, when he sees his glitter bum, starts rubbing at it furiously with his towel. I'm glad that Mum's not offering to help. She just stands there giggling and pointing.

Then he does what he does in class, when he can't take a joke. He gets nasty.

'*What's so funny?*' he yells at us.

This makes Mum collapse with laughter.

'Tell me, *what's* so funny?' he keeps yelling, his voice going higher and higher.

'Oh, Graham!' she says, trying to pull herself

together, 'it's just a bit of glitter on your bottom! But it does look funny! Ha ha ha!'

He looks as though he could swipe her with his towel, but then he suddenly changes his mood and says, 'OK, OK, the joke's on me. Now let's have that swim.'

As he follows her through the door he turns and throws me an *'I'm-going-to-get-you-for-this'* look.

I respond, much to my surprise, in a totally un-professional way. I mean, it's the sort of thing that secret agents are *not* supposed to do. I stick out my tongue. To which he gives me the finger.

See? Nasty!

I watch them stroll down to the jetty and when they get on to it, he does a really mean thing. He pushes Mum into the water. Hat, sandals, sunglasses and all.

'Now look who's funny!' I hear him laughing like a maniac.

He offers Mum his hand but she refuses his help. Instead, she lifts herself on to the jetty, dries herself and sets back to the house.

'Oh, come on, can't you take a joke?' I hear him calling after her.

I've not much time. I must launch my next mission without delay.

Operation Pong

I dash upstairs to his room. On his chest of drawers is a row of fancy bottles. I open up a few and take a whiff. One with a wolf's head on the label is called 'Le Loup'. Poo! It smells like tobacco – a smell I can definitely improve on!

Neatly arranged over a stand are some clothes – his outfit for tonight, I guess. White trousers, white shirt, white socks and *another* white thong – all 100% jerk. I peep through the window. They're standing halfway between jetty and house, in deep discussion. I dash to my room and collect a few items from my arsenal.

A few seconds later, I'm back in his room. Quickly, I open a stink bomb capsule and empty a few drops into his cologne, turning 'Le Loup' into 'Le Poop'.

Next:

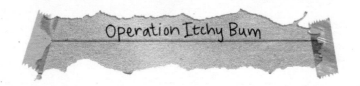

Operation Itchy Bum

I lightly dust his thong with itching powder. Then, with the footwork of 007, I skip back to my room.

Operation Pong

← itchy powder

silly thong

stink bomb

Operation Itchy Bum

Stage 1

Stage 2

I'm all
smiles when they
come up to say hello.

'What's up, Al?' Burke the Jerk asks, as
though everything's been swept under the
carpet.

'All sorted,' I say. He'll soon know what's up,
all right!

Up his silly thong!

Chapter Ten

Mum's the first to notice.

'Poofy! What's that?' she asks, as we drive to the Captain's Table.

'Manure,' says Graham. 'They spread it on the fields at this time of the year. Wind up your window, darling.'

Darling … *darling!!*

Mum winds up her window, and the smell of rotten eggs and tobacco grows even stronger.

'Someone's let off!' I yell from the back.

'Don't be crude, Alistair!' snaps Mum. But I

see her give him a sideways glance, and delicately clamp her nose. *She thinks it's him!*

I'm gagging by the time we pull up at the Captain's Table. I leap out of the car and fan fresh sea air into my nostrils. Mum takes a deep breath and says, 'I thought I was going to die in there!'

Burke the Jerk, unbothered by the pong hanging about him, locks the car and leads the way. I hang back, waiting for Operation Itchy Bum to kick in. He walks jauntily beside Mum and makes a big fuss about opening the door for her. Just before slipping through himself, I notice him giving his bottom a good scratch. I catch up and follow them to our table.

The first scratch must have set off a fierce reaction because as we approach our table he clenches his bottom and almost trips.

'Are you all right, Graham?' Mum asks.

'Fine, fine,' he snaps, digging into his butt so fiercely that he misjudges his seat and falls on to the floor. A waiter rushes over and helps him to his feet. Beads of sweat have gathered on the Jerk's forehead and he looks as though his red face might explode.

Suddenly Operation Itchy Bum shifts into top gear.

Screek! Screek! Screek!

He starts scraping his bottom like a dog on a carpet – backwards and forwards on his chair.

'Whatever is the matter, Graham? You look … stressed out,' says Mum.

'I … I … aaaahh!' he starts uttering, then suddenly leaps up, clutching his buttocks. He looks as though he wants to tear them apart as he dashes to the men's toilet.

Bewildered, Mum says, 'Please see what's the matter with Graham, Alistair.'

I get up slowly and, taking my time, stroll to the men's toilet. I give the door a push with my foot and go inside. Lying in a basin is Burke the Jerk's mangled thong.

'Sir … oh, Grahaaam!' I start calling.

'Aaaaaaah, aaaaooh!'

I follow the groaning and sound of splashing water to a closed booth.

'Graham?' I call, tapping on the door.

'Everything OK in there?'

 'Ooooeeeeoooh aaaaaahheee!'

'Well, we're waiting for you to order,' I say.

'Eeeeaaaaarrgh,' he answers.

'Righto! See you inside,' I say. Then, with a hop, skip and jump I'm back at the table.

'Is he all right?' asks Mum.

'I think he's got something wrong with his bum.'

'Oh, Alistair D'Arcy McDermott, you're awful!'

I can't disagree with that. So I keep quiet and look at the menu. Think I'll skip fish and go straight for the dessert – chocolate-covered ice cream!

When Burke the Jerk finally makes an appearance, he's not a pretty sight. His hair hangs in strands over his forehead. Behind, his hair extension has formed itself into a stringy mullet, and he looks as though he's lost his appetite.

'Would you prefer to go home, Graham?' Mum asks kindly.

Too exhausted to speak, he nods.

I lick my spoon, and we leave.

Mum drives. But halfway home she has difficulty seeing where she is going because of some bright lights following behind. I turn around and recognize the same van as before.

Chapter Eleven

One day down, two to go.

I don't think he suspects me.

When I join them for breakfast, I hear him say:

'It was terrible, like some allergic reaction.'

'Washing powder ...' says Mum. 'Some brands can be quite fatal.'

'I guess I'm lucky to be alive,' he says, bending over to kiss her. He's fully recovered. When he sees me he says brightly, 'That was really nice of you to come to my rescue last night, Al.'

'How's the bum?' I ask.

Mum chokes, 'Alistaaaaair!'

'It's fine, fine, fine,' he says. 'Bum's fine.'

He's being as cool as a snake. Mum gives him
a warm smile. They must have made friends
again last night.

So, time to get cracking on my next mission.
While they make plans for the day, I take my
bowl of cereal upstairs, open my book and
write down my plans for:

Operation Sabotage

First, I do a time study on Burke the Jerk's
morning habits.

8.00: gets up
8.05: takes a dump
8.30: feeds his face
9.00: showers

There's no time to lose! I hear the shower
going and gather my sachets of tomato and
mustard sauce. Mum's downstairs washing
breakfast dishes.

I tiptoe to his room and enter. The bathroom
door is half closed. I have a few seconds to
complete my mission. I pull open a couple of

sachets of each, give
them a little tear,
and place them near
the tip of each of
his canoe-size
shoes. Then leave
as I came – in silence.

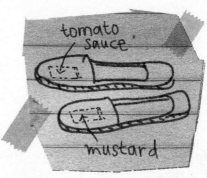

Back in my room I wait. I hear the shower
stop. Shuffle, shuffle … more shuffling … some
happy whistling. Then it comes:

'What the … *bleeeeeep*!'

Mr Burke doesn't use that word!

I peep into the passage and see Mum rushing
to his room.

'Just look at my … *bleeping* shoes!' he yells.
'Paid a fortune for these. They're genuine
Antonio Banderas espadrilles!'

'They look fine to me,' says Mum. 'What's
the fuss?'

'Look, inside! See? A bloody mess! And what's this!'

He's discovered the sachets because I hear him yell:

'Tomato sauce sachets! It's vaaandalism! Your *bleeping-butter-wouldn't-melt-in-his-mouth* son planted these!'

'For heaven's sake, Graham, it's a little practical joke. Kids do this to each other all the time,' Mum says, trying to calm him down.

'Well, I'm not a bleeping kid!'

'Then stop acting like one, and I'll have a word with him.'

I dash to my bed and pretend I am reading the book picked up from my table.

'Put down that Bible and look at me,' says Mum, marching in.

I look at her, as though butter wouldn't melt in my mouth.

'Did you put tomato sauce in Graham's espadrilles?'

'What are espadrilles?' I ask, playing for time.

'These!' She sticks his big shoes under my nose.

'Oh, thooose!'

'Well, did you?'

'Tomato sauce?' I ask, playing for more time.

'Alistair D'Arcy McDermott, did you or did you not put sachets of tomato and mustard sauce into Graham's Antonio Banderas espadrilles?'

'Well, not exaaactly,' I answer. 'You see, there are tomato sachets and there are mustard sachets, but I've never heard of or seen tomato AND mustard sachets.'

'Stop it, you hear me!'

I do – I quit fooling around and listen. She means business. Speaking slowly and steadily she says, 'I'm really disappointed by your attitude.

Ever since we've arrived, you've been trying to wreck this weekend for me. And if you pull off another trick like this, I'm going to send you to a school where boys your age shave!'

I'm really shocked. My own mother threatening to send me to such a school …
a school for boofy boys!

Then I think, cos you've gotta think at times such as these:

She DID say 'another trick like *this*'. And as I've already done with *that* one, *technically*, I guess there are *other* kinds that I might be free to use?

That's what always gets you off in a court – being found 'not guilty' on *technical* grounds.

I must be looking quite sweet and harmless with these thoughts running through my head, because Mum softens and says, 'I'm glad we've had a little talk. Now let's put this behind us. Get your cap and sunscreen. We're going fishing!'

As we walk down to the jetty, Burke the Jerk stops, takes off one of his espadrilles and inspects his toes.

'Oh, look, Graham,' says Mum, lightheartedly. 'You've got tomatoes. Get it? Toma-toes!'

'Yes, funny … very droll … very punny!' His feeble attempt at a joke makes Mum laugh. They're still too chummy for my liking. I reckon it's time for –

But out on the water, it's so peaceful that I almost forget I'm at war. Mum and Burke the Jerk sit up front where he gets stacks of opportunities to paw Mum as he shows her how to attach the bait to her hook. I lounge at the back, where I study the workings of the motor – just in case I have to get Mum and myself across the sea to safety. I look over the bay and spot a boat that appears to have a film crew on board. From a distance they seem to be filming us. But Burke the Jerk is so involved with fishing and flirting that he doesn't notice them.

Suddenly, Mum's rod jerks into action and she screams, 'I've got one! I've got a BIG one!'

'Steady,' says Burke the Jerk and puts his

arms around her, helping her pull in her catch. As the poor fish flaps out of the water and is swung into the boat, he kisses her neck. I turn away and hear a motor start up. The boat with the film crew approaches us, then makes a wide turn and heads across the bay.

'Look, Alistair! Look what your brilliant mother's brought in. We'll have a fish barbecue tonight!' yells Burke the Jerk, holding up the catch. I give him the thumbs-up, pull the ignition cord, and shout:

'Man overboard!'

Chapter Twelve

'I really don't know what's got into you, Alistair,' says Mum, helping Burke the Jerk on to the jetty.

'Sorreeee,' I say.

'It's not me you should be apologizing to,' Mum snaps back.

'Sorreeee, Grahaaam!'

'Poor Graham,' says Mum. 'We must get you out of these soaking clothes.'

When we get inside, Mum removes his shirt, and he steps out of his wet trousers.

'Sit down while I get these shoes off,' says Mum.

'Espadrilles!' corrects Burke the Jerk.

'Well, whatever they are, I can't get them off,' she says, tugging at them like a Rottweiler at the end of a rope. No go! No budge! She makes several more attempts – all useless.

Burke throws his head back, covers his eyes and moans, 'Get them off, get them off!'

'His shoes are shrinking! Maybe we'll have to cut off his feet!' I gasp, lending a hand. Burke gives me a withering look. Mum looks pooped. Suddenly, I get this idea where I can appear helpful while earning extra time to launch into my next mission.

So I say, 'We need some gel to get these big boats off his feet.'

'Espadrilles,' murmurs Burke, looking ready to pass out.

'Brilliant idea!' says Mum, and I skip upstairs.

There, I throw myself into my next mission:

Operation Pussy Paws

All you need is:

A chocolate bar – always have one of those ✓

A rubber pussy-paw stamp – got it ✓

Method:

Lick the chocolate bar until it's nice and sticky

Press against rubber stamp and...

START WALKING!

By the time **Operation Pussy Paws** is completed there's nothing left of the chocolate bar, and it looks as though some rogue pussy has had a nice stroll across Burke the Jerk's big white bed. Before I slip downstairs, there's time for one more mission – maybe the last:

Operation Green Teeth

All you need is:
Some green food colouring — got it ✓

Method:
Drop two drops (don't overdo it!) onto enemy's toothbrush

His toothbrush is one of those multi-bristle jobs so the green colour isn't very noticeable.

green food colouring

'Alistair! Where's that gel?' Mum calls from below.

'Coming!' I shout, giving my mouth a wipe. I return the food colouring to my backpack, pick up the gel from my arsenal, and go to the rescue.

A few dabs around Burke the Jerk's big feet, and Mum is able to shift, then slide them out of the soaked espadrilles.

'They're ruined,' sighs Burke the Jerk, holding up his limp shoes.

'I'll buy you another pair,' says Mum.

'Oh, you are a sweetums,' says Burke the Jerk, pouting his lips.

Then he hands me back my gel and says, 'Thanks … *for nothing*!'

'Why don't you rest, Graham?' says Mum.
'Alistair and I will take a little walk along the
beach.'

I pull a face.

'No arguments!' says Mum. 'We need to talk.'

Actually, I'm rather glad to be out of there
before Burke the Jerk gets to his bedroom.

★

The sun is starting to set as Mum and I reach the beach. I wish it *was* only us two here … and Dad. Mum puts her arm around me as we walk along the shore.

'You've been a bit of a beast, you know, Alistair,' she says softly.

'It's just …' I start, wriggling out of trouble.

'I know. It's just not working,' she replies. 'Graham doesn't seem to like children, which is strange when you think that he's a teacher.'

'He *hates* children, Mum,' I say.

'He certainly hates his job,' Mum says. 'In fact, he has as much as said that if we got married he'd like to give up teaching.'

'Married!' I shriek.

'Yes, he's been talking about it a lot. Only, I'm not at all sure I want that for us, after seeing him overreact to your silly pranks.'

'He's psycho, Mum,' I rub it in.

'Let's say he's a bit *strung-out*. Teaching must be a stressful job. Still, he seems to have a very short fuse.'

I wish she wasn't so understanding! I wish she'd see right through him – so that we can go back home and never see him again.

But standing in the golden light of the setting sun, she looks sad. And I *really* do want her to be happy. The way she was when we were all on holiday in Venice … when she and Dad were still in love.

I hear her sigh, 'It's so beautiful here.'

We watch the sun hanging gold and heavy over the horizon. The sea laps gently over sand and shells. The seagulls seem to have finished their feeding for the day. Just a few stragglers noisily make their way home, high up on the cliffs.

'Beautiful … and so peaceful,' says Mum as she takes my hand and we turn back to the house …

… where peace has been sent packing by Burke the Jerk.

We are met by him as we arrive – holding up his big used-to-be-white bedspread like a curtain for us to see as we arrive. He looks as though he is about to spit razor blades.

'Now this!' he yells. 'Tell me, *will this terrorism never end*?'

I quickly cover my tracks. Now *that's* punny. Get it? My tracks?

'It must be the cat that came through the window earlier on,' I say. 'I thought it belonged to you. It was … sort of … white … white-ish … with dark … chocolate paws,' I let slip.

'Oh, Graham,' says Mum, 'let me see that?'

Rudely, he flings the bedspread at her.

'This'll come clean,' says Mum, examining the marks. 'I'll give it a wash tomorrow. Come on, let's all relax and start a fire for our fish barbecue.'

She leads Burke the Jerk by the hand into the house. He goes to a cabinet and pours himself a large, long drink. Then offers Mum something, and to me he says nastily:

'What do hyperactive little brats drink?'

Mum doesn't hear him. If she did I bet she'd give him a piece of her mind.

'Coke,' I say, not wanting to get into a fight right now.

He throws a can across the room to me, just short enough for it to hit the floor. When I open it, it fizzes all over me.

'Nice catch!' he says, grinning from ear to ear with those big white teeth of his. That makes me smile – when I think of how green they will soon be.

Mum comes in carrying the fish wrapped in foil for the fire.

'Nice to see you two getting along,' she says, seeing us smiling our different smiles.

Now, praise where praise is due – Burke the Jerk makes a seriously good fish barbecue, with the taste of the sea in every bite. In fact, sitting on his patio with yummy smells drifting off the barbecue, I am not interested in launching another attack on my enemy this evening.

I've heard of English and German soldiers doing that. In the First World War on Christmas Day, they laid down their arms and had a game of football – laughs and all. The next day they were blowing each other's brains out. Weird! But that's what's happening right now. I've called a truce.

★

After dinner, a game of Trivial Pursuit is suggested.

'Goody!' says Mum. 'I love holiday games.'

We each choose our colours and the game starts.

We play for a while, with Burke the Jerk leading. So far, he's been lucky to get lots of history questions. Then the tables turn and I take the lead. I notice Mum, who's really bright, hanging back – allowing me to win. This causes Burke the Jerk to fidget, suck his teeth … sigh … tug at his chest hairs, and crack his knuckles. Mum and I exchange looks. I think she's starting to see through him at last.

A few minutes later, Mum has fallen well behind, leaving Burke the Jerk and me head to head … with one remaining question between us.

It's my turn to answer!

I roll – a science and nature question.

I notice him lick his lips before asking the question:

'Who invented the word "robot"?'

I pretend to strain over the question, muttering, 'Ooh, that's a tough one.'

'You can't take forever on this,' he complains.

His eyes are beady with expectation.

Then I give it to him, 'The Czech author Karel Čapek!'

He can't believe that I got it correct. That I've won!

'Sorrrrreeee,' he says, 'you've got that one wrong.'

'No I haven't!' I argue. 'Mum, look at the answer!'

'Hand it over,' says Mum, holding out her hand to Burke the Jerk.

Guess what?

He smacks it away, and holds the card behind his back!

'Hand it over,' says Mum, sternly. 'I want to see if you're cheating.'

'CHEATING!' he spits out. 'Ridiculous. I'm a member of Mensa International!'

'Then you ought to know the rules of a simple child's game,' says Mum. 'Show me the card!'

Suddenly, a scramble breaks out. Mum is all over him, trying to wrestle the card out of his hand. But before she can get it, he does the most unbelievably dumb thing. He starts chewing it up! Mum lets go her grip … and comes away with his hair extension in her hand! We burst out laughing. He looks like a chicken that has had its back quarters plucked. Infuriated, Burke the Jerk leaps up, spits out the pieces of card and roars:

'GET OUT! GET OUT OF MY HOUSE!'

'For heaven's sake,' says Mum, handing him back his hair. 'It's far too late for us to leave now. We'll go in the morning. And frankly, Graham, I don't think I want to see you again.'

He grabs his hair from Mum and storms off to his room. We hear him doing a lot of *bleeping* up there. And then finally it goes quiet.

Mum looks at me and says, 'Guess you were right, he is a jerk.'

★

Mum suggests that we get up before Burke the Jerk wakes up, and head for home.

'I'm going to bed now. I feel as though I've been caught up in a horrible movie,' she says.

I'm too hyped-up to sleep, so I switch on the TV and watch some rubbish called *Trashy Two-Timers*. It's a reality show that uses cameras to expose people who cheat on their partners.

I watch for a few seconds, yawning my head off … then I see it – the van! It's the same one that's been hanging around our road; the same one that followed us from the Captain's Table. I

 stay glued, as the camera team follows a big unshaven loser who's two-timing his hysterical wife.

They bust him and his poor wife's best friend while he's smooching and stuffing his face with sushi.

The cheating couple look as though they've been attacked by men from Mars.

His wife's best friend is like … WHAAT!

His furious wife wants to pull his head off.

It's too awful. I switch off and go to bed.

We're out of here tomorrow!

It's amazing how much nervous energy I've used up on all my missions.

I don't buy Agent 007 getting all lovey-dovey after a big mission of wiring, bombing, ducking flames, rolling in dust, diving off the sides of cliffs, being washed out to sea, wrestling with man-eating sharks, and finally pulling himself on to a land-mine-infested beach. No way! He'd have to go on holiday with Gran and her old ducks to recover.

Images of Gran and 007 begin to swirl in my mind until I nod off.

In my dream, a green-toothed dragon thrashes about on a sandy beach. He stamps and stamps, but his big white espadrilles remain stuck to his feet. In his fury, he explodes, sending bits of dragon meat flying through the air.

Then Gran and 007 wash up on the beach. Gran's in a bikini.

'Bloody hell, James,' says Gran. 'We got here too late for the action.'

Chapter Thirteen

I wake up with a start. Mum is shaking me like
a life saver trying to revive a drowned man.

'Come on, we've got to get out of here!'

It's morning, and she's already packed. I
jump out of bed in the clothes I slept in and
gather my things. We meet on the staircase,
trying not to make a sound. But the staircase
creaks like an old ship, sounding louder because
we are trying so hard *not* to wake up Burke
the Jerk.

'Damn!' says Mum. 'He's locked the door.'

We put our things down and start looking for a key.

I think I hear him moving about in his room.

'Hurry, Mum!' I whisper.

She returns from the kitchen with a bunch of keys.

'Here, I've got it!'

She tries one … but it doesn't turn.

'Try that one, Mum!' I say, pointing to any old one.

'You're making me all flustered,' she snaps back.

'That one, Mum!' I splutter.

She tries it … and it works.

We pick up our things and scramble to the car. I wait for Mum to open up, but she's standing looking like someone who's seen an ogre – *a green-toothed ogre*!

'Oh no!' groans Mum, dropping her car keys.

Burke the Jerk *comes storming towards us*! Nostrils flared, lips flapping and green teeth gnashing. We can't hear what he is shouting, but it sounds *verrry* threatening.

Mum grabs my hand and we run towards the jetty. I'm glad that I got to know the engine of Burke the Jerk's boat. We are going to have to make a sea escape – if we can get there in time!

The rest feels like a slow motion movie:

He is shaking me. Mum's shouting. I strike out against his attempts to take me by the throat and throttle me. Then, as though there's a sudden channel switch, we are surrounded by a camera team and some heavies who move in quickly to restrain Burke the Jerk. He's gone completely off his rocker and wants to beat up everyone. In the confusion, a big blonde in a pink tracksuit pushes through the crowd ... Miss Merchant!

Now I've heard Miss Merchant do LOTS of voices. But NEVER the spine–chilling, blood-curdling scream of an avenging banshee:

'YOU TRASHY, LOW-LIFE, DRAIN-SOILED, DIRTY PIECE OF TWO-TIMING DONKEY DUNG – WHO DO YOU THINK YOU ARE CHEATING ON!!!!'

Suddenly, we are on *Trashy Two-Timers*!

Burke the Jerk is ranting in a green-toothed babble that nobody can understand. Miss Merchant is standing with his hair extension in her hand. It looks as though it has been dragged backwards through a shredder. When she sees me she says tearfully, 'I'm so sorry about this, Alistair, but that miserable piece of pig snot has been two-timing me long enough.'

Mum explains that she had no idea what he was up to. I decide not to remind her that I had *told* her about Miss Merchant. It's messy enough.

'We were supposed to be getting married next week,' sobs Miss Merchant. 'He told me he was having his stag night this weekend.'

Mum comforts her. 'How terrible. You're much too nice for him.'

'And so are you,' says Miss Merchant. 'Men are such dogs!'

'Hey!' I want to say. But just then an old red-headed woman pushes her way through the crowd. When she learns what's going on, she lets Burke the Jerk have it –

'What's wrong with you, you despicable, shoddy excuse for a man?' she hollers. With each insult she delivers a clout with her big beach bag.

She's his old mum who actually owns the holiday house!

The cameras are all over us.

Miss Merchant cheers up, touches up her make-up and faces the camera, looking like a tragic, but beautiful, star in a tragic, but trashy, movie.

Mum holds my hand with one hand and covers her face with the other.

And me?

I stand smiling.

Mission accomplished!

Chapter Fourteen

It's taken Mum a long time to recover. Mostly she's angry with herself.

'How could I have been so stupid?' she asks Gran.

'Easy,' says Gran. 'Men are rats.'

'Hey!' I say. 'Some men are like Dad and me … sweet and good.'

'You're sweet, for sure,' says Gran. 'But after what I've heard about that weekend, I'm not sure if you're good.'

'He saved me from that horrid man,' says

Mum, giving her hero a hug.

'I wonder what happened to him?' says Gran.

Well, I guess you want to know too. So here's what happened:

After the nasty exposure on TV, *Mr Oh-So-Sorry-for-Cheating-on-You* Burke the Jerk left Obz. It turns out that besides Mum and Miss Merchant, he was dating a Miss Trixie Le Page, who has five o'clock shadow and speaks in a deep voice.

'He disgusts me,' she told the reporters.

After her appearance on TV, Miss Merchant got a role in a daytime soap. I watched once … and she's *amazing*!

Then one night, Mum yells for to me come and see what's on the box.

I rush in, just in time to catch … the one and only Burke the Jerk on screen.

Can you believe it!

Burke the Jerk has become the new presenter for *Trashy Two-Timers*!

Mum and I roll about. But, seriously, we're *really* glad he's on the box and not in our lives any more.

In fact, after the Burke the Jerk affair, Mum is much happier with the life she has with *me, me, me*!

School still sucks.

And I still spend weekends with Dad, who had a very successful business trip and has moved into a new apartment. No 'C' view, but state of the art! He's joined a team on an enormous project – the BioDome – a megalithic glass dome, all steel girders and glass, taller than the London Eye. It has its own eco-system with an indoor Japanese tea garden – waterfall, lake, swans and all. I swear! I've seen it! Well, almost all of it that's been finished so far. Dad introduced me to some of the engineers on site.

'Is this your kid who plays "Mull of Kintyre" on the bagpipes better than that McCartney geezer?' they wanted to know. 'Great kid you've got there, McDermott,' they said.

Dad beamed, and I didn't know where to look.

As we walked home to his new apartment he said, 'Want a piggyback, Al?'

Of course, I gave him my 'no way' look.

'Guess you're too big for that now?' he laughed.

I am. But I still like being read to and tucked in at night.

Like now …

'So, how are things at school?' he asks.

'Sucks!'

But that's not *really* the truth, because I won a merit award at the Caber and Bagpipe Schools Festival. And while I see a little less of Sophie, I've started hanging out with Julian Pettifer, whose parents *are* together. I'm included in all their nerdy interests – like going to computer fairs, looking at interesting websites, making a blog and exploring other possibilities on the internet.

In fact, it's Julian who encourages me to use computer technology for my final mission.

I consider it to be the most important one …
the most challenging … the most dreamt-of:

Operation Anonymouse
('cause no one will ever guess who's behind it, see.'

This is how it works:

With a little help from Julian, I write the
following email on his computer –

```
To whom it may concern:
THIS IS NOT SPAM SO DO NOT DELETE!
You are invited to tea at the Japanese
tea garden in the BioDome at 3.00 p.m.
this Sunday. See you there! Good tea
and fortune awaits your fine company.
Yours totally sincerely,
Anonymouse
```

We read it. Julian says, 'You don't spell—'
But before he can finish what he's saying, I
click on the send button and out it goes …
to Mum and Dad.

*

When I can, I check Mum's inbox. It's been received! Of course, being signed 'Anonymouse' means that she's not going to know who it's from.

'What do you think, Mum?' she asks Gran. 'It sounds like some online-wacko looking for a date.'

'I would have thought you were through with blind dates,' says Gran.

'No, no – you must go!' I pipe up. Their heads turn, like aliens sensing an intruder in their midst. I carry on: 'Anonymouse sounds so genuine … don't you think?'

'Alistair D'Arcy McDermott,' says Mum. 'I've told you not to read my email!'

Gran winks at me then turns to Mum. 'Listen, I'll go with you. That way you won't be strangled by Mr Anonymouse.'

Good old Gran!

Mum takes out her diary and writes aloud, 'Tea … three thirty.'

'Three …' I correct her, '… this coming Sunday.' She looks up.

'At the Japanese tea garden, left of the bridge,' I add.

'You seem to know quite a lot about it,' she says.

'The BioDome,' I remind her.

I catch Gran smiling as though she's on to me.

Dad's not letting on. By Saturday, I'm curling up with curiosity. So after lunch, I ask, 'What are you doing tomorrow, Dad?'

'Working,' he says.

'No, no! You're always working. How do you expect to ever MEET anyone! DO anything! GET A LIFE!'

He looks blankly at me.

'I had a life, once,' he says, as though he's talking to himself. 'Didn't realize how much I miss it. Want something to drink?'

He goes to his state-of-the-art kitchen to pour juice. While he's away I swing over to his laptop and open his email. I scroll down the inbox. Anonymouse is not there!

Blast!

'Here you go?' he says, handing me a glass of juiced blackberry. Remember, I told you he's hopeless with food, but he's really great with juice. It's real crushed blackberries made with his cool juice extractor.

'You know that Japanese tea garden at the BioDome,' I say casually, licking the fruity ring around my mouth.

'Yep,' says Dad. 'It's been packed ever since the BioDome opened this week.'

'Well, I'd really like to go there sometime.'

'We can do that now,' he says.

'What about tomorrow?'

'I'm working. I told you.'

'But it's Sunday! Everyone spends time with their kids over weekends. You've got to *prioritize*, Dad.'

That's a Julian word. I rub it in. 'You're wasting me, Dad! All over the world, dads are doing cool things with their kids … going to parks … feeding swans … *prioritizing*.'

'OK, OK … message received … it's in the inbox … being processed!'

'So can we go?'

He looks at me as though I'm a ton of bricks waiting to be fork-lifted.

'OK, you're on,' he says finally.

I bully him into writing it down. He goes to his laptop.

'3.00 p.m., tomorrow,' I instruct him, adding, 'Japanese tea garden!'

'Funny,' he says, looking up. 'That rings a bell. Oh yes, some junk mail I deleted yesterday,' he mutters.

Junk mail! I especially wrote DON'T DELETE!

He can be *soooo* annoying!

'Call Mum and ask if you can stay and have lunch with me tomorrow,' he says.

'Not lunch! We are having tea … at three!' I yell. He looks at me as if he doesn't know what I'm getting all hissy about. Honestly, sometimes I think he's losing it: little things, like going out with shaving cream on his chin. Sometimes he even forgets to shave! I've really got to start keeping an eye on him.

'Lighten up!' he says, throwing me his mobile. I speed-dial home.

'Anything the matter?' asks Mum when she hears me.

'No, but can I stay a bit later with Dad tomorrow?'

She pauses, and I overhear her say to Gran, 'You're still on for tomorrow?' Murmur, murmur – then:

'That's fine. What are you guys going to be doing? Something special?'

'Very special,' I say.

Wooah! Just the thought of it makes me want to lift off the ground.

'Like what?' she asks.

'Sorry Mum, you're breaking up,' I lie.

Click!

'Time for bed,' says Dad, leading me by the shoulders. He lifts the duvet and I climb in. He reads a bit of *Goodnight Mister Tom*. It's sad in places and the boy, Will, reminds me of myself. We can smell the coffee and still put up a fight. When he finishes, he switches off the light and bends over to kiss me goodnight.

I run my finger across his prickly chin.

'Dad,' I say. 'Promise me something.'

'Come on then,' he says.

'Tomorrow when we go for tea, will you shave?'

He smiles. 'Sure thing, Al my Pal.'

I watch him slip into the bright light of the passage. I miss the old red night-club light of Dad's old flat. His new place is really big and glitzy. Mum would like it a lot. I imagine them chatting in the passage.

'I love him more than anything in the world,' says Mum.

'There's nothing I would not do for him,' says Dad.

I close my eyes and go to sleep.

Chapter Fifteen

Sunday, and it's a horrible grey day. But I want to leap into the air and stay there. Today's the day!

'Looks like a day to stay indoors?' says Dad, peering out of the window.

'The BioDome *is* indoors,' I remind him, running my eyes over his stubbly chin.

'Don't worry, I'll shave,' he says. 'After breakfast.'

He lines up a selection of cereals – he's SOOOO good at cereals.

I munch loudly through some new invention – little round oaty biscuits – SCRUNCH, SCRUNCH! – like a gerbil.

Dad looks up from his coffee and grins; says nothing – just grins.

'Whaaa?' I ask with a mouthful.

'I love having you here,' he says, grinning from ear to ear. 'Wish you didn't have to go home.'

I'm working on that!

'Can I call Mum?' I ask.

'No need to ask,' says Dad.

'Hi, Mum?'

'No, it's Gran.'

'Hi Gran, where's Mum?'

'She's popped out to pick up a new dress. Anything I can do for you, darling?'

'No. I was just checking that she hasn't forgotten about …' I quickly check that Dad can't hear, 'you know, the invitation to the Japanese tea garden.'

'No, she's not forgotten about it. That's what the new dress is all about.'

'Gran?'

'Yes.'

'Do you know what's up?'

'What do you think … Mr Anony-Mouse?'

'Oh, Gran! What about Mum?'

'I think she was very moved by your email. I think you've done a rather daft but very wonderful thing.'

I can't think of anything to say.

'Are you there?' asks Gran.

'Yep.'

'Well, see you later,' she says and ends the call.

Dad comes out of the bathroom looking like
Mr Smooth. But he's wearing an ancient
college sweater. I get him to change it.

'I look like a gondolier in this,' he complains.
'You look like a dork in the other one,' I say.
'I am a dork,' he replies.

'No you're not!' I argue.

'I'm a dork for leaving your mother,' he says.

I hand back his college sweater.

'You're a dork,' I agree with him.

On the way to the tube I skip ahead, calling, 'Come on! You walk so slowly!'

'What's the rush?' Dad calls back.

Everything!

The smell of rain in the air, an autumn breeze on my flushed cheeks, the crowded tube that will take us to the BioDome. It all feels like one enormous rush of happiness to my head.

'Come on!' I yell, jumping off the tube as soon as the doors open.

'Come on!!' I moan, tugging his sleeve, as we walk through a gentle shower towards the BioDome.

And guess what?

It's summer in the BioDome!

We make our way through the crowds to the Japanese tea garden and find a table. I order cold apple tea with cherry ice. Dad orders a tea with floating rice-paper water lilies.

'Who are you looking for?' asks Dad.

I realize that I've been swivelling in my chair, looking out for Mum and Gran. I settle down facing him.

'Just looking,' I say.

But I'm starting to worry. Where are they? Has Mum got the details all confused? Is Gran holding her back in those big high-heel clumpy shoes of hers?

A Geisha lady arrives with our order and I start fishing out the cherry ice-balls.

Suddenly, Dad's expression changes.

'There's Mum and Gran,' he says, getting up.

I turn around and wave to them.

Mum's looking really smashing. Her new dress is more beautiful than all the Japanese lanterns strung together. She approaches us looking like a shy girl on her first date.

'Will you join us?' asks Dad.

'Sarah will,' says Gran. 'Alistair and I will take a walk.'

This isn't going as planned. I imagined myself sitting between the two of them where I could give them a good talking-to – tell them to stop being so stupid and miserable, that we should all try to be as happy as we were that time in Venice when Dad bought Mum the red wine glass that she still uses, and Mum got the stripy top for Dad that makes him look like a gondolier.

'Alistair!' barks Gran. 'Up!'

She pulls me out of the chair, with the spoon still in my mouth.

'We're going to look at swans,' she says. 'See you two later.'

Gran takes me by the hand down a winding path that leads to a little bridge over a lake. There we stop and she rests a hand on my shoulder as we watch a family of swans glide beneath us.

'Why did Mum and Dad fall out of love, Gran?' I ask.

Gran catches her breath, then says, 'I think they got married too young – straight out of university. Then you came along a year later and … well, I think they just did not have the time to be kids.'

So I *was* to blame!

'No one's fault,' says Gran. 'That's just the way it happened. They love you and that's what really matters.'

'But do you think they could fall in love again, Gran?' I ask.

'Maybe,' says Gran. 'Your mum certainly acted like a love-struck girl going to have tea with her boyfriend. Thank heavens it wasn't a blind date. I've had enough of those!'

I smile. 'So she knew who Mr Anonymouse was?'

'Well, not at first. Your mum's a bit thick in certain ways, if you don't mind me saying,' says Gran. 'I had to give her a few clues. Your spelling finally gave you away. Anyway, I don't want you to get your hopes up too high. We must wait and see.'

As we walk back to the tea garden, the light changes – from a bright summer afternoon to a balmy summer evening. High above, a full moon hangs in a holographic sky.

'Bizarre!' says Gran, removing her shawl.
'What next?'

Well, when we look towards the tea garden,
we see Mum and Dad holding hands. They look
serious, but when they see us, they smile.

'How are the swans?' Mum asks.

'Their babies are quite big,' I start telling them.

'But still needing Mama and Papa swan,' says
Gran.

I notice a quick exchange of secretive looks.

'Sit down. We've something important to tell
you,' says Dad.

Told you! Didn't I?